DEREK JETER

PRESENTS

NIGHT at the STADIUM

by Phil Bildner

illustrations by Tom Booth

ALADDIN JETER CHILDREN'S

New York   London   Toronto   Sydney   New Delhi

ALADDIN JETER CHILDREN'S

An imprint of Simon & Schuster Children's Publishing Division • 1230 Avenue of
the Americas, New York, New York 10020 • First Aladdin hardcover edition April 2016
Text copyright © 2016 by Phil Bildner • Illustrations copyright © 2016 by Tom Booth
All rights reserved, including the right of reproduction in whole or in part in any form.
ALADDIN is a trademark of Simon & Schuster, Inc., and related logo is a registered trademark of Simon &
Schuster, Inc. • For information about special discounts for bulk purchases, please contact Simon & Schuster Special Sales at
1-866-506-1949 or business@simonandschuster.com. • The Simon & Schuster Speakers Bureau can bring authors to your live event.
For more information or to book an event contact the Simon & Schuster Speakers Bureau at 1-866-248-3049 or visit our website at
www.simonspeakers.com. • Book designed by Laura Lyn DiSiena • The illustrations for this book were rendered digitally. • The text of this book was set
in Burbank. • Manufactured in the United States of America 0316 LAK • 2 4 6 8 10 9 7 5 3 1 • Library of Congress Control Number 2015953870
ISBN 978-1-4814-2655-8 (hc) • ISBN 978-1-4814-2656-5 (eBook)

For Anna and Audrey

–P. B.

THE YANKEES WIN!

"That was the awesomest game ever!" Gideon cheered.

"Time to get some autographs!" Dad said. "Follow me."
Gideon loved collecting autographs. His autograph book
was filled with signatures.
But one was still missing—
the autograph he wanted
more than any other.

"Everyone stay together,"
Mom said.
"You hear that, Gideon?"
his sister, Audrey, added.

As Gideon's dad led the family down the aisle, Gideon reached into his pocket and . . .

OH NO!

His autograph book was gone. He turned to look for it, but suddenly the crowd pushed him away.

He bounced off backpacks,

pinballed off purses,

and ducked under diaper bags.

Finally, Gideon bumped into a door.

He stumbled and staggered in.

He zigged up one ramp . . . .

and zagged down another.

Hello? Anybody here?

Up ahead, Gideon spotted some shadows—*moving* shadows.

He looked for somewhere to hide, but there was nowhere to go but forward.

"What are you doing here?" said a voice.

All Gideon saw was the groundskeeping equipment. He blinked hard.

"YOU TALK?"

"Of course we talk," the hoses said.

"We all talk," said the rakes.

"Some of them talk too much," said the hoses, spraying the rakes, "and they need to stay away from *our* outfield and stop messing up *our* grass!"

The rakes pointed their tines. "They need to stay away from *our* infield and quit muddying *our* dirt!"

"Excuse me," Gideon said, interrupting the argument. "I need to find my family. Can you help me?"

"Why didn't you say so?" one of the rakes said. "Go down this hall and . . ."

One of the hoses squirted
the rakes . . . again.

How would
you know?

Gideon didn't know where he needed to go,
but he knew he needed to find his family.

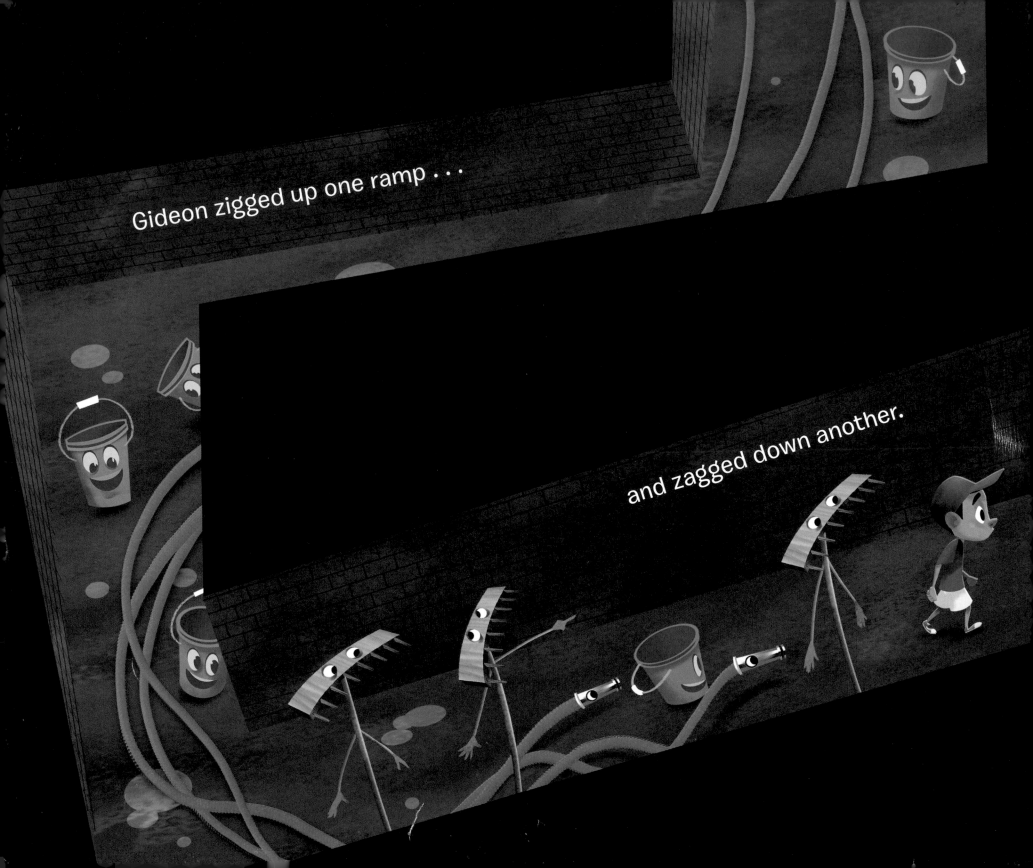

Gideon zigged up one ramp . . .

and zagged down another.

Gideon ducked as a baseball whizzed by his ear. "You talk too?"

"Of course we talk!" the balls said bouncily.

"We all talk!" the bats added woodenly.

"We play, too," the bases boasted.

A bat leaped into Gideon's hand.

You're up, kid!

All of a sudden Gideon was playing baseball with the baseballs, and the bats and bases too!

Gideon took several mighty swings, and then he remembered his mission.

I need to find my family. Can you help me?

"Why didn't you say so?" said the gloves. "We'll give you a hand. Go down those stairs and—"

"No!" the bats cracked. "You go up these stairs and—"

"How would you know?" the balls said, bobbling. "You bats are always in the hitters' hands, and you gloves are always on the fielders' hands. We go everywhere!"

Gideon still didn't know where he needed to go, but he knew there was no point in listening to gloves, balls, and bats bicker.

As Gideon zigged up one ramp and zagged down another, he heard more voices up ahead. . . .

"Talking food?" asked Gideon.

"I need to find my family," Gideon said. "Can you help me?"

"Why didn't you say so?" the cotton candy said. "Go to this corner and—"

"*No*," the peanuts said. "Go to that corner and . . ."

The hot dog sprayed ketchup and mustard everywhere.

"We all know where to go to see the one person who can help this boy find his family." The hot dog shook its buns. *"MONUMENT PARK!"*

Gideon pushed open the door and stepped into Monument Park.

"I was waiting for you," a voice boomed.

"A talking monument?" Gideon blinked. "A talking Babe Ruth monument?"

"That's right, Gideon."

4 3 5 7 37 8 8

Gideon pointed to himself.

"You know my name?"

"I know everything about this place. I also know everywhere that everyone needs to go." He pointed to the other end of Monument Park.

Gideon blinked hard. Then he blinked even harder. Standing right in front of him . . . was the Captain, Derek Jeter.

"I was waiting for you, Gideon," he said.

"Waiting for me?" Gideon asked.

I have something that belongs to you.

He pulled out Gideon's autograph book. "You're still missing a signature. May I?" The Captain signed his name right on the front cover.

Thanks, Mr. Jeter.

Suddenly Gideon's family raced into Monument Park. "There you are!" Audrey shouted. "You're in *big* trouble!" "We were worried about you!" his mom said. "Where have you been?"

"You won't believe what happened," Gideon said. "Meet my new friends." He ran over to the doorway. . . .

But there was nothing and no one.
"I'm telling you, you won't believe . . ." Gideon stopped.

Even he didn't quite believe his night at the stadium.